Victor Moves

The Sound of V

by Joanne Meier and Cecilia Minden • illustrated by Bob Ostrom

The Child's World

Published by The Child's World®
1980 Lookout Drive
Mankato, MN 56003-1705
800-599-READ
www.childsworld.com

The Child's World®: Mary Berendes, Publishing Director
The Design Lab: Design and page production

Library of Congress Cataloging-in-Publication Data
Meier, Joanne D.
  Victor moves : the sound of V / by Joanne Meier and
Cecilia Minden ; illustrated by Bob Ostrom.
      p. cm.
  ISBN 978-1-60253-420-9 (library bound : alk. paper)
  I. Minden, Cecilia. II. Ostrom, Bob. III. Title.
PE1159.M47 2010
[E]—dc22   2010005609

Printed in the United States of America in Mankato, MN.
July 2010
F11538

NOTE TO PARENTS AND EDUCATORS:

The Child's World® has created this series with the goal of exposing children to engaging stories and illustrations that assist in phonics development. The books in the series will help children learn the relationships between the letters of written language and the individual sounds of spoken language. This contact helps children learn to use these relationships to read and write words.

The books in this series follow a similar format. An introductory page, to be read by an adult, introduces the child to the phonics feature, or sound, that will be highlighted in the book. Read this page to the child, stressing the phonic feature. Help the student learn how to form the sound with her mouth. The story and engaging illustrations follow the introduction. At the end of the story, word lists categorize the feature words into their phonic elements.

Each book in this series has been carefully written to meet specific readability requirements. Close attention has been paid to elements such as word count, sentence length, and vocabulary. Readability formulas measure the ease with which the text can be read and understood. Each book in this series has been analyzed using the Spache readability formula.

Reading research suggests that systematic phonics instruction can greatly improve students' word recognition, spelling, and comprehension skills. This series assists in the teaching of phonics by providing students with important opportunities to apply their knowledge of phonics as they read words, sentences, and text.

This is the letter v.

In this book, you will read words that have the **v** sound as in: *very, moving, seven*, and *visit*.

4

Victor is very happy!

He is moving to a new house.

It is seven hours away.

Victor will make new friends. He can also visit his old friends.

It is fun to move. Victor puts every toy in a box.

The movers put every box in a van. They drive the van to the new house.

Victor and his mother ride

in their car.

Victor waves to the big trucks. Some of the drivers wave back.

Victor sees the new house.

It is very big. He loves it!

Victor gives his mother a big grin. He never wants to move again!

Fun Facts

Vans come in all sizes. Some vans are the perfect size for a family. Does your family have a van? Some vans need to be larger to carry mail or packages. Vans carrying food to restaurants and grocery stores can be very large. A moving van is one of the largest vans on the road. Do you know how much a moving van weighs when it is full of furniture and boxes? It can weigh about 10,000 pounds (4,536 kilograms)!

Imagine moving west in a covered wagon. Moving during the mid-1800s was much different than it is today. Most people moved in small farm wagons because they were much easier to maneuver. Children could take only one or two small toys. Most of the space in the wagon was taken up by clothing and food. A family of four needed 1,000 pounds (454 kg) of food to survive the journey to Oregon or California.

Activity

Building a Playhouse with Moving Boxes

Do you think boxes are just for moving or storing things? Use moving boxes to construct a playhouse. You can even put two or three boxes together to make a playhouse with more than one room. Ask a parent to help you if you need to work with scissors to cut the cardboard. When you are finished making your playhouse, decorate it with crayons or markers.

To Learn More

Books
About the Sound of V
Moncure, Jane Belk. *My "v" Sound Box*®. Mankato, MN: The Child's World, 2009.

About Moving
Harper, Jessica, and G. Brian Karas (illustrator). *I like where I am*. New York: G. P. Putnam's Sons, 2004.
Maisner, Heather, and Kristina Stephenson (illustrator). *We're Moving*. Boston, MA: Kingfisher, 2004.

About Vans
Ernst, Lisa Campbell. *This is the Van That Dad Cleaned*. New York: Simon and Schuster Books for Young Readers, 2005.
Maestro, Betsy, and Giulio Maestro (illustrator). *Delivery Van: Words for Town and Country*. New York: Clarion Books, 1990.
McKay, Sandy, and Meredith Johnson (illustrator). *The Big Tan Van*. San Francisco: Treasure Bay, 2001.

Web Sites
Visit our home page for lots of links about the Sound of V:

childsworld.com/links

Note to Parents, Teachers, and Librarians: We routinely check our Web links to make sure they're safe, active sites—so encourage your readers to check them out!

V Feature Words

Proper Names
Victor

Feature Words in Initial Position
van
very
visit

Feature Words in Medial Position
drive
driver
every
give
love
move
mover
moving
never
seven
wave

About the Authors

Joanne Meier, PhD, has worked as an elementary school teacher, university professor, and researcher. She earned her BA in early childhood education from the University of South Carolina, and her MEd and PhD in education from the University of Virginia. She currently works as a literacy consultant for schools and private organizations. Joanne lives in Virginia with her husband Eric, daughters Kella and Erin, two cats, and a gerbil.

Cecilia Minden, PhD, is the former director of the Language and Literacy Program at the Harvard Graduate School of Education. She is now a reading consultant for school and library publications. She earned her PhD in reading education from the University of Virginia. Cecilia and her husband, Dave Cupp, live outside Chapel Hill, North Carolina. They enjoy sharing their love of reading with their grandchildren, Chelsea and Qadir.

About the Illustrator

Bob Ostrom has been illustrating children's books for nearly twenty years. A graduate of the New England School of Art & Design at Suffolk University, Bob has worked for such companies as Disney, Nickelodeon, and Cartoon Network. He lives in North Carolina with his wife Melissa and three children, Will, Charlie, and Mae.